PREACHER MAN

Volume 1
The Devil To Pay

Murray Pura

Copyright 2014 Murray Pura ©

First Edition

Published by

Helping Hands Press

ISBN: 978-1-62208-510-1

Printed in the United States of America

PROLOGUE

An American military base
Somewhere in Germany
December 2012

There were no windows in the room and no doors.

The two men had entered using an elevator shaped like a ball that came up through the floor and disappeared back the way it came.

Staff called it Get Smart.

The men faced each other on either side of a white table.

The walls were white, the chairs were white, the overhead lighting was white.

The older man had his reading glasses on, wore a light gray suit that was the same color as his hair and skin, and was scanning documents that appeared one after the other on a laptop that faced him.

The younger man had dark brown hair and dark brown eyes, was about six three, slender and muscular, and wore white overalls. He kept his eyes on the older man, said nothing, and waited.

Finally the older man sat back in his padded white armchair and stared at the younger man.

"Ten years of exemplary service," the older man finally said.

"Thank you, sir."

"Chasing the devil and his minions all over God's green earth." The older man removed his reading glasses. His eyes were as gray as his suit and hair. "Do you believe in all that hocus pocus?"

"It doesn't matter if I do or not, sir. The devil worshippers stake their lives on it."

"Hm. And presumably their eternal souls." The older man steepled his fingers under his chin. "They'd certainly like to send Dirk Austen to hell if they could get their hands on him."

"I'm aware of that."

"You've killed or incarcerated cult leaders in France and Switzerland and the UK and everywhere else. This despite the fact these men and women were protected by powerful politicians in Berlin and Paris and London. And Washington and the UN."

"Not to mention the Vatican and Jerusalem, sir."

"Not to mention." The older man kept his eyes fixed on the younger man. "All under the guise of a naval chaplain who enjoyed the privilege of serving our Navy Seal teams. And as a special agent with the State Department and the Diplomatic Security Service who went by the code name Preacher Man and worked out of our embassies all over the world. Considering the sort of demons you fought in the field, never mind in the State Department and the Navy Chaplaincy Corps, it's a wonder you're still intact, body and soul."

"Angels on my shoulder, sir."

"I thought there were only fallen ones in the corridors of power."

"You'll find both kinds there, sir. If you could speak to any of the Satanists who are behind bars I believe they'd tell you they found an encounter with pure light a far more frightening experience than any of their encounters with total darkness and depravity."

"I have spoken with them." The older man's gray eyes narrowed. "They hate you with a hatred I have never seen before, not even in the eyes of the most fanatical religious zealot or cold-blooded terrorist."

"I try to keep my emotions out of it."

"I suppose that's why you were so successful in shutting down their Black Masses and Black Sabbaths and all their attempts at global domination."

"That and prayer."

"Prayer? So you do believe in the hocus pocus?"

"I believe in God."

"Well, then God must have believed in you and your cause because here you are sitting in The White Room with me today." The older man unsteepled his fingers. "Once you leave this room, Special Agent Dirk Austen will cease to exist."

"I know, sir."

"The threat level against you is too high and the danger of you being caught and interrogated too great. Have you met with the surgeons?"

"Yes, sir."

"Have you come to an agreement on what you would like to look like?"

Austen nodded.

The older man smiled. "I wish it were me going under the knife. I could come out looking twenty years younger. Have all the beautiful female federal agents my heart desired."

"I've sworn an oath under the Espionage Act to remain single, sir, and unattached emotionally and sexually. It would be high treason to break that oath."

"Yes. And all that nasty celibacy makes it sound as if you were some sort of warrior monk fighting those devil worshippers all those years."

"I suppose I was."

The older man stood up, put his hands in the pockets of his suit pants, and began to pace the small room, eyes on the walls and floor. "Once you have recovered from the plastic surgery, once the swelling has gone down, there will be an extensive series of photo ops. We will create a short but honorable career in the United States Navy Chaplain Corps for you. Abruptly terminated by your refusal to stop using the name of Jesus Christ and God at military funerals and military worship services. That sounds like something you might have done anyways so it shouldn't be too hard for you to play along."

He waited for Austen to respond, but the young man remained silent.

The older man continued to pace. "You will have a new life and a new past. The procedure will be similar to the Witness Protection Program. You will have no further contact with anyone you knew in the Foreign Service, the special ops groups, or the Navy Chaplain Corps. Not that it matters much. Even your eyes will be altered. No one will recognize you. Except me. And you will never hear from me. When my replacement takes over I will brief him in as skeletal a fashion as possible."

"Why brief him at all, sir?" asked Austen.

"Because there is the chance, the slight chance, a need may arise that is so severe we require your skill set again, your skill set and your faith. In that case you will be tapped to return to active duty as a covert agent. But I hope that won't be necessary. It's my belief all this mumbo jumbo Satan worship and Illuminati nonsense has had its day and the need for a vampire hunter like yourself, if you'll pardon the comparison, is at an end."

"Where am I going with my new identity, sir?"

"Montana. You will candidate for the position of lead pastor of a Baptist church with about three hundred souls and you will get it. With the Rocky Mountains over your shoulder you will spend the rest of your days preaching sermons, visiting the sick in the hospital, marrying and burying, and providing pastoral care and counseling to your flock. It will not compare with tracking down devilish men in dark suits and devilish women in black dresses who have bodyguards that look like the angel of death."

"If I can go fishing and hunting and horseback riding it will be a welcome change, sir."

"Hm." The older man stopped pacing and gazed at Austen. "I pray you'll never need it, but you'll be provided with a satellite phone no bigger than the palm of your hand that will only activate in response to your voice, your sweat, your fingerprints, your body heat, and pulse, and eyes. It will only work with your living tissue. Should a call come through on that phone it will be heavily encrypted. Should you need to make a call on that phone it will be heavily encrypted. Encryption codes will change hourly. That doesn't concern you. But if the phone is ever used you will be in direct contact with myself at State, with the President of the United States, and with one other person."

"Who is that?"

"I'm not at liberty to say."

"Does the President get briefed on my continued existence under a different identity?"

"Yes, he does. By me. Now that he's won his second election I will be having a sit down with him in the new year. There will be other matters to discuss as well." The older man was standing by Austen's chair. "If anyone else tries to use the phone it will go dead. And I'll know. Keep it in a safe place. Check it every day."

"What about batteries?"

"It has a power source that lasts over a hundred years. Do you intend to hang around any longer than that?"

Austen smiled for the first time. "My code name was never Methuselah."

"No." The older man suddenly thrust out his hand. "It was a pleasure to serve with you, Special Agent Austen. Godspeed."

Austen gripped the hand. "Thank you, sir. All the best back at State with your own particular brand of demons."

"I could use your holy water and crucifix when I fly back there after your surgery."

The older man crossed back to his side of the table. He pressed something under the tabletop. Within moments the round bulletproof elevator with its white steel frame emerged from the floor in a corner of the room. Two guards in white tactical uniforms and helmets and assault rifles stepped out and waited. Austen smiled for a second time because the two soldiers were noticeably black in the all-white environment.

Austen walked over to the elevator. "Sergeant Smith. Sergeant Jones."

They nodded.

"Sir."

"Sir."

He stepped into the elevator and they joined him.

"Are you going to miss seeing my face around here, Sergeant Smith?"

"No, sir."

"How about you, Sergeant Jones?"

The sergeant cracked a smile. "It will be a refreshing change of scenery, sir."

"Thank you, thank you very much."

"You're welcome, sir."

Austen had one last look at the older man in the gray suit before the elevator sank below the surface of the floor.

"I do believe," he said.

1

Blue Sky Community Baptist Church
City of Diamondback
County seat
Anaconda County, Montana
January 2014

Καὶ ἐγένετο πόλεμος ἐν τῷ οὐρανῷ, ὁ Μιχαὴλ καὶ οἱ ἄγγελοι αὐτοῦ τοῦ πολεμῆσαι μετὰ τοῦ δράκοντος. καὶ ὁ δράκων ἐπολέμησεν καὶ οἱ ἄγγελοι αὐτοῦ, καὶ οὐκ ἴσχυσεν οὐδὲ τόπος εὑρέθη αὐτῶν ἔτι ἐν τῷ οὐρανῷ. καὶ ἐβλήθη ὁ δράκων ὁ μέγας, ὁ ὄφις ὁ ἀρχαῖος, ὁ καλούμενος Διάβολος καὶ ὁ Σατανᾶς, ὁ πλανῶν τὴν οἰκουμένην ὅλην, ἐβλήθη εἰς τὴν γῆν, καὶ οἱ ἄγγελοι αὐτοῦ μετ᾽ αὐτοῦ ἐβλήθησαν.

"And there was war in heaven," the man murmured to himself at his oak desk. "Michael and his holy angels battled the dragon and his dark angels. But the dragon and his angels were not strong enough to defeat Michael and the holy ones and the dragon and his spawn were hurled out of heaven. The great dragon fell, the one we know as the ancient serpent, the devil, the adversary, accuser, slanderer, deceiver, seducer, persecutor, liar, tempter, the god of this world, the prince of the power of the air, the spirit of lawlessness, ruler of demons, Lord of the Flies, Lucifer, son of the dawn. This is the evil one who lures the entire world into darkness, depravity, and death. He fell, and fell, and fell, like lightning flashing across a sky of storm clouds. And his angels, broken and hateful, fell with him. And so they came to earth. This is the spirit of Anti-Christ that is already among us. So we know it is the last hour."

The man tapped his fingers on the well-worn pages of his Greek New Testament.

"A rather free translation," he admitted, still looking down at the Greek printing. "But it's a true translation, just the same."

He picked up his cup of coffee. It was still warm. Leaning back, he sipped at it and glanced at the wall. His secretary, tired of waiting for him to do it, had framed and put up his large ordination document with all its fancy calligraphy. He could barely make out his name there were so many loops and curls to the letters.

Reverend Jude Aaron Blackstone

Not far from the framed document was a small mirror he used to comb his hair and adjust his tie before weddings, and funerals, and Sunday morning worship services. He could see his face clearly in it – hair as black as a raven's wing, eyes as blue and sharp as the Montana sky in winter, high cheekbones tanned mahogany from cross country skiing and snowshoeing, a chin that looked as if it had been chiseled out of cold granite. He made a face at the image.

I am Dirk Austen. But who are you? I'm living in someone else's body and I can never get out.

There was a quick rap on the door to his study.

"Pastor Jude?"

A tall woman of about fifty entered the room. Her face was bronzed by hard ranch work in all kinds of weather and lined by years of rough wind that carried an edge. Long sun-colored hair had been brushed to a gleam and knotted into a braid that fell halfway down her back.

"What's up, Crystal?" asked Blackstone.

"I wanted you to know the Greek Orthodox priest in Missoula called, Father Daniel. He's on the road and expects to be here for the ministerial meeting at eleven."

"Dan's going to make it? Great. I haven't seen him since Thanksgiving."

Crystal looked at an orange sticky in her hand. "The Lutheran minister from here in Diamondback called to confirm too. And the rabbi from Beth Shalom. The Pentecostal minister said he would see you next week when the evangelical ministerial has a potluck at his home."

"All right. Whatever."

"Then there was a strange call from the Catholic priest, the new one."

"He's only been here a month. I haven't even met him yet." Blackstone watched as Crystal continued to scan the sticky. "What was so strange about the call?"

"He said the Wednesday paper had just come out and you needed to read it. The front page."

"I didn't even listen to the radio this morning. What's in the paper that matters so much?"

"They hadn't dropped it off when I checked our mailbox half an hour ago. Do you want me to take another look?"

"No, I'll go. I need some air." Blackstone got out of his chair. "You can turn on the local station and we'll compare notes."

"Will do."

Blackstone threw on his fleece and went outside. The church building was tucked up close to a pair of hills and just beyond them the Rocky Mountains. He headed across the large gravel parking lot towards the white peaks. The morning sun had cleared the rocky slopes and shone directly into his eyes.

He was back in the French minister's massive office with its tall windows, its gold encrusted ceiling, and its ornate furniture that predated the French Revolution. The sun had been shining into his eyes at exactly the same angle, at the same time of day, and with the same winter sharpness.

"Certainly the Paris police will assist you with your investigation, Monsieur Austen." His dark hair combed back with every hair perfectly in place, the man had given him the smile of a hawk. "And of course I will extend every courtesy of my office."

"Your police have actually done everything in their power to hinder my work."

"I am sorry to hear you say that. I assure you I will look into your allegations and give the matter my personal attention."

"That must be a very old ring on your finger."

The minister had not dropped his eyes from Austen's. "Why do you say that?"

"I recognize the design and the stone. It's medieval. Unless it's a clever reproduction you are wearing a piece of jewelry hundreds of years old, perhaps as much as six or seven hundred."

The minister had smiled. "It is not a reproduction."

"How did you come by it?"

"It has been in my family for generations."

"Really? Because that ring is reserved for Grand Masters who perform the ritual of the Black Mass. They are said to be second only to Satan himself in terms of earthly powers."

The minister's smile remained in place.

"How does it go?" Austen had begun to recite the Black Mass in Latin. "You probably know those words better than I do."

The smile was gone. "Do not speak those words here. They are only for the ritual. In the proper place, at the proper time, after all the preparations have been made. You soil them by bandying them about in public."

"I didn't think it was possible to soil words that were already filthy with blasphemy and hate."

"You consider it blasphemy, you with your twisted god and his twisted cross. I consider the words sacred. They are real power. Stop wasting them."

But Austen had carried on. Squinting into the morning light from the windows, the French minister had seemed to Austen to come and go, to be solid and substantial one moment, and a slender column of black light the next.

"You mock us." The minister's voice rasped. "You hunt us. Somehow you have the idea in your head that you have power over us. But you don't. We control the capitals of the world and their governments. At our whim nations rise and fall and wars are begun and ended. Your prayers and worship do nothing. Hasn't your frustration with your god taught you how powerless he is by now? In my hands and in the hands of others of my Order is the destiny of America and the EU and China. We will decide who lives and who dies, who is saved and who is damned. The power rests with us. And with Our Master." He had paused to lift his hand so that the ring flamed in the sunlight. "We will break you and all like you. You hunters will become the hunted. I look forward to the day I offer you up as my morning sacrifice to my Great Lord, the Son of the Dawn."

Blackstone pushed the memory to the back of his mind.

The French minister had been burned to death in a fire in the ancient dungeons beneath the building. The fire had never been explained nor had the coroner ever seen the charred remains.

The mailbox was at the far end of the parking lot. Austen pulled out several large envelopes.

Diamondback, Anaconda County

Not for the first or last time, Blackstone wondered why the county had used those names. The closest diamondbacks were in southern Idaho, this county only saw prairie rattlers. And the closest anacondas were thousands of miles away in South America.

"Well," he said out loud, "I suppose a few snakes that don't belong wander in now and then."

The newspaper was rolled up and stuffed in the box. He pulled it out and shook it open.

THIRD BODY FOUND IN WOODS

A jagged coldness made its way into his chest and head.

"The first was the Catholic priest in November," Crystal reminded him back at the office. "The second was that homeless man just before Christmas. Now we have a third murder. Sheriff Parker will be pulling his hair out."

"We don't know that any of them were murders, Crystal." Blackstone poured himself a second cup of coffee. "The priest's death was ruled a hunting accident."

"It's easy enough to make a killing look like a hunting accident, Pastor."

"The Sheriff's Office never said foul play was suspected."

"The Sheriff's Office never said anything one way or the other. Doesn't it strike you as suspicious how little they have to say about these deaths? Even now they won't identify the latest victim."

"They have to notify next of kin first. That's standard procedure."

"I just hope you and the other ministers will pray about all of this."

"Of course we will." Blackstone glanced at his wristwatch. "They'll start arriving in ten or fifteen minutes. I should check on the coffee. What about donuts and apple fritters?"

"I'll nip out and get a dozen."

"Thanks."

Crystal headed for the front doors and Blackstone went with her part of the way.

"Don't be frightened," he said. "The Sheriff's Office will figure this out. If the deaths are related it will eventually come to light. Prayer will help bring clarity."

"I hope so, Pastor."

"If there is a connection it can only be hidden for so long. I ought to drop by and tell Sheriff Parker he has our support and blessing."

Crystal had her hand on the door. "That's not a bad idea."

Just as she said this a patrol car with a sheriff's gold badge on its side pulled up in front of the building.

Anaconda County Sheriff, it said under the badge. *Preserve and protect.*

The sheriff stepped out of the car. He was a tall, heavy man in a black Stetson wearing a black leather motorcycle jacket lined with white fleece. He did not remove his aviator sunglasses as he pushed against the glass doors and entered the church.

"Sheriff Parker." Crystal covered her surprise with her biggest smile. "We were just talking about you."

"I hope it was all good."

But he did not smile in return.

"You can be sure it was, Bill," she told him.

"Nice to know."

Blackstone extended his hand. "Sheriff."

Parker took the hand. "Reverend."

"Crystal is telling the truth," Blackstone said. "We *were* talking about you. I want you to know you have our church's prayers and support as you deal with this latest death."

The sheriff nodded. "Thank you." He removed his Stetson. His hair was cut as close to the scalp as possible. "That's why I'm here. My own minister said you would be meeting here today with the others. Reverend Frank Lucas."

"Holy Redeemer Lutheran. I didn't know that was your home church."

"Used to go to Mass. But Jessica was raised Lutheran and she missed it. Now that the kids are grown up and gone we decided to make a change. No offense."

Blackstone shook his head. "So long as you honor Christ as Savior and Lord, I don't care where you go, Sheriff. Frank is a good man. Loves his people and loves God."

The sheriff nodded. "I appreciate that." He looked around. "Where's the meeting taking place?"

"In the church lounge at eleven. Did you want to say something to the ministers?"

"If that's all right."

"It's perfectly fine. Let's wait for them by the fire."

"I'll just get those fritters." Crystal leaned against the door again. "Anything special for you, Sheriff Parker?"

"I haven't had much of an appetite today." The first trace of a smile moved over his lips. "But a maple donut might go a long way to fixing that."

"A maple donut it is. I'll be back in two shakes."

Blackstone walked with the sheriff to the lounge. "That body in the woods must put a lot of pressure on you and your deputies."

"You have no idea. The phone's been ringing off the hook. They're even calling my cell. People think the deaths are related and that a serial killer is on the loose."

"How did this person die?"

But the sheriff didn't answer Blackstone's question. "That's a nice looking gas fireplace."

"Thank you. We had it put in after the first cold snap."

"Jess and I were thinking of getting one installed. Waiting for a sale."

"Wait another couple of months till spring and they'll be sixty per cent off."

"Trouble is, we won't need it anymore come spring." Parker settled into an easy chair by the fire. "Does everybody usually come to these meetings on time?"

Blackstone nodded. "We share for about half an hour and pray for about half an hour. Everyone has a bag lunch and we supply coffee and dessert. Can I get you a cup?"

"Please."

"Black?"

"Please. I hope it's strong as iron."

"One thing I've never learned to do is make coffee weak. Sometimes the spoon stands up straight."

Parker gave a quick laugh. "Glad to hear it. Tell me, how long have you been in Diamondback now?"

"Two years this Easter."

"How's that been for you?"

"No regrets. I have a fine congregation here."

"You're what, thirty, thirty-one?"

"Thirty-two."

"Confirmed bachelor?"

"Looks like it."

"There are some mighty beautiful women in Anaconda County. Good Christian women."

"I guess I've been too busy to notice."

"Sheriff Parker." A short and slender man with a trim beard, black fedora, and dressed in a black suit came into the lounge. "It's good to see you here."

Parker got to his feet and shook the man's hand. "Rabbi."

The rabbi shook Blackstone's hand as well. "I didn't know we were having a guest. What's the occasion?"

"He dropped by to have a word with us."

Parker returned to his seat by the fire. "I need to ask the clergy for their help."

The rabbi took the armchair next to him. "Help with what? A fundraiser?"

"The killings."

"Killings? When you put it that way you make it sound as if the three people were murdered. I thought the priest's death at least was accidental."

Parker finally removed his sunglasses. His eyes were a cold, hard green.

"It wasn't," he said.

Both Blackstone and the rabbi stared at him but did not respond.

Over the next few minutes the others arrived – the Orthodox priest, Father Daniel from Missoula, who was an hour's drive from Diamondback; the Lutheran minister from Holy Redeemer, Frank Lucas; the United Methodist pastor, Brent Scott; and the new Roman Catholic priest, Father Eric. Sheriff Parker briefly asked for their help with the criminal investigation and invited them to drive across the city to the morgue and meet him there. They left their lunches in the church fridge and brought their coffees, donuts, and apple fritters with them. Rabbi John Cohen had a van so all of the ministers piled in. John followed the sheriff's patrol car.

The coroner met them there. He was dressed in his white lab coat.

"I realize you have seen any number of bodies as you helped members of your congregations prepare for funerals," he began. "But I must warn you that this is not anything you have seen before."

He led the ministers and Sheriff Parker to the room where he performed his autopsies. There was only one body on a table and it was covered up. He glanced at the men and drew back the sheet.

The dead man was on his stomach. But his head was twisted around 180 degrees. Naked face, back, buttocks, and legs stared at them. His tongue was extended far out of his mouth and a five-point pentagram cut into it.

"Oh, my God." Brent Scott sank into a metal chair near the table.

The coroner spoke quickly. "Bruise marks on both sides of the neck and jaw suggest the victim was seized by the head and that sufficient strength was applied to break the neck and twist the head completely around."

"Who has that sort of strength?" asked the Orthodox priest, Father Daniel. "Even a bodybuilder would find that difficult to do."

"In the movies they show people doing that sort of thing all the time," said Frank Lucas.

"In the movies, yes, anything is possible in Hollywood." Father Daniel's face was pale. "In the real word it is not so easy."

"There is the matter of the pentagram," Father Eric the Catholic priest spoke up. "Either it was a Satanic ritual or someone wants us to think that way."

"We've never had ritual abuse in Anaconda County, at least not any the law was made aware of." Parker held his black Stetson in his hands. "Generally you saw more of that in the 80s and 90s right across the country. Are any of you gentlemen privy to information about devil worship or covens or witchcraft in the area?"

"I haven't heard a thing," responded Cohen.

"Neither have I." Father Daniel ran his hand through his thick dark beard. "Not a word."

Parker glanced at Brent Scott who was still seated in the chair. Scott shook his head.

"Does anyone know the dead man?" asked Father Eric.

"No," replied Parker. "And his wallet was gone. No ID. But a ten dollar bill and some coins were lying beside him in the snow."

Cohen folded his arms across his chest. "You don't apply superhuman strength and twist a head all the way around to steal a wallet and leave the cash behind."

Blackstone spoke for the first time since the coroner had exposed the body. "Do you think there's a connection with the other deaths?"

The sheriff and the coroner exchanged a look.

"Put the pictures on the board, Sam," Parker said.

The coroner picked up a large manila envelope from a nearby counter and stepped up to a bulletin board. He began to attach nine by twelve color prints to the board.

"This is Father Henry's body," explained Parker. "Taken at the scene of the hunting accident as well as here at the morgue."

The blood left Father Eric's face.

The body was dressed in hunting cam. It was on its stomach with the head twisted around 180 degrees so that it faced backwards just like the corpse on the table. The tongue was extended and a pentagram carved into it. In all of the pictures dried black blood crusted around the mouth and down the jaw to the throat. In one the eyes were still open in a scream.

"That's enough for me." Brent Scott got to his feet. "I don't know how you think we can help you. Whoever did this needs a shrink. And a padded cell."

"Are you sure you don't know anyone involved in Wicca or voodoo or black magic?" asked Parker.

"Wicca wouldn't do this."

"You haven't heard of any devil worshippers gathering in the hills or mountains?"

"In the dead of winter?" Scott pointed angrily at the photographs of the dead priest. "Henry was a good man. Look, there is no devil, so all this talk of ritual abuse is nonsense. You have to find someone who likes to kill. Don't get thrown off the track by the pentagram." He walked swiftly from the room. "I'll wait outside."

The others watched him leave.

The coroner was placing new photographs on the board.

"This was the second victim," said Parker. "A few days before Christmas. We were never able to establish his identity. His wallet was gone just like this one. And the cash was left behind in the same way."

The body on its stomach. The head twisted around so it faced backwards. The extended tongue with a pentagram cut into it. The dried blood all over the lower part of the face and throat and chest.

The rabbi, John Cohen, blew out his breath in one long exhalation. "The citizens of Anaconda County don't know anything about this."

Parker's face was set like rock. "It was my call. I didn't think anyone needed to know how the priest had died. We launched an investigation. When the second body showed up the same way we figured we might have a serial killer. But I didn't want to spread panic. Not at Christmas. I had my deputies scour the murder scene and the countryside for clues. It's almost the end of January. Whoever had done it I hoped had moved on."

"What are you going to do now?" asked Cohen.

"Come clean. Tell the county we're treating the three deaths as homicides. That the manner in which each person was killed leads us to believe the men were murdered by the same individual or individuals. Ask for help. Now the priest is the only person we've been able to identify. Even though we composed the face of the Christmas victim so that it was presentable, and placed photographs of him in the paper, no one came forward. Sheriff's Offices across Montana and Wyoming and Idaho have the pictures but there's still nothing. We have no idea why these men were killed. Of the three, Father Henry appears to be the only one who was a local citizen. Perhaps he was in the wrong place at the wrong time. Perhaps he was in a part of the forest where the killer had a tent or lean-to. His death may not have been planned. The murderer might just be targeting drifters and the priest was the odd man out."

"Was there any sign of a tent or lean-to?" asked Father Eric.

"No, there wasn't."

"Did Henry have his wallet on him?"

"Yes. Full of cash."

The priest shook his head and rubbed his hand over his face. "None of it makes sense."

"Unless they actually were sacrifices of some sort." The Orthodox priest Father Daniel shrugged. "We can't rule that out, can we?"

"You don't believe in the devil and demons and all that exorcism stuff, do you?" Frank Lucas demanded. "The killer just did that to put the sheriff off the scent."

"Then why were they murdered?" retorted Father Daniel. "Nothing was stolen from the priest or the others. Exceptional force was exerted to break each neck and twist it around. Why bother doing that? Why bother with the pentagram? They could have used a knife or a gun."

"They're sick. Brent is right. Sick and ugly and badly in need of counseling and therapy." Lucas almost glared at Sheriff Parker. "You'll take heat for holding back the truth."

Parker's face darkened. "We never knew what the truth was, pastor. We still don't know what we're dealing with. Do you want a city gripped by fear? It's not a pleasant experience. People see demons under every bush and they start shooting innocent men and women just for stopping them on the street and asking directions."

"Do you have any leads?" Blackstone interrupted the flare-up between Parker and the Lutheran minister. "Any at all?"

Parker looked around at the group of pastors. "We have so little to go on. I'll get criticized for my handling of the information and how much we released to the public. I can shoulder it. But I kept hoping we'd get a break, some bit of evidence that would clear the air and give us something we could tell the papers and the citizens of Anaconda County. All we can do is advise them to lock their doors and avoid strangers. None of that will help if the killer isn't a stranger."

"Are you going to tell them about the manner in which these men were murdered?" Blackstone asked.

"No. And neither are any of you. That information stays with the Sheriff's Office and the coroner."

"What about the people who found the victims?"

"Deputies found the priest and the Christmas victim. The woman who discovered this latest body has sworn to us she'll keep it to herself. Said she didn't want to talk to anyone about it anyways." Parker placed his Stetson on a counter. "Look. If you hear anything, anything at all, about someone dabbling in black magic or Satan worship, I don't care if they believe in it or not, you tell me. One last thing – the only clue we have so far, and I mean the only clue, is footprints at this latest crime scene."

"What kind of footprints?" Father Eric asked him.

"Those of a very light and very petite woman. A size four and a half boot."

"Weren't there any boot prints by Father Henry?"

"He'd been dead for days before the deputies found him. There'd been a storm. The only tracks they found were those of the coyotes and foxes who'd been gnawing on his body." Parker looked deliberately at Frank Lucas. "Something else we have no intention of sharing with the public."

"And the Christmas body?" pressed Eric.

"Found in a ditch and covered in snow. The only reason the deputies spotted him was a bunch of crows had gathered to peck at his eyes and face. At first Carson and Selleck thought it was road kill."

"A size four and a half boot." Blackstone brought the conversation back to the footprints. "Can you take a cast of it? Is there anything distinctive about the tread?"

"Yeah, we have a couple of casts. Got Carson trying to get a fix on brand and style. I think it'll turn out to be just another Walmart snow boot. Nowhere to go with that."

"You think a tiny woman snapped these victims' necks?"

Parker shook his head. "No, I don't. But in this case I think a woman found the victim shortly after his death and kept it to her self. If we tell the public we have footprints at the scene perhaps that'll spook her enough to get her to come forward and tell us what she knows."

"Maybe she saw the killer," responded Blackstone. "That would be reason enough for her to want to keep her mouth shut. She wouldn't relish being hunted down and turned into the next cold body."

"We should go." Lucas began to head towards the door. "Brent's waited for us long enough. There's nothing we can do here. Let's get back to the church, have our lunch, and spend some time in prayer. That's the best we can do."

"Sure. Don't forget to eat lunch. Don't forget to pray." Parker almost sneered at Lucas. "Don't any of you believe real devil worshippers could be involved? That these victims could have been offered up to Satan?"

Lucas made a sour face. "Maybe the killer believes it. But I doubt it. He's just trying to confuse you, sheriff, and he's doing a good job."

"I believe it," said Father Eric. "It's clearly taught in Scripture. Whether the killer is a devil worshipper or not, I have no idea at this point. But there are people out there who choose to worship Satan and Satan accepts their worship and empowers them in whatever ways he is permitted."

"Oh, come on, Eric," sputtered Lucas.

"I believe it too." Father Daniel put his hands in his pockets. "The devil and the occult are real."

"Well, I am with you and Father Eric on that." Rabbi Cohen put his black fedora back on his head. "I'm not sure what I think of magic spells and people in hoods chanting in Latin and pentagrams. But if we don't believe the supernatural breaks into the natural world how can we believe in God?"

Lucas made a sound that was part groan and part sigh and headed out the door.

"What about you, Pastor Jude?" Parker turned his gaze on Blackstone. "Where do you stand in all this?"

Blackstone lifted one shoulder in a half-hearted shrug. "I like the quote by the Irish writer, Oscar Wilde – *We are each our own devil and we make this world our hell.* I believe that covers all the bases when it comes to your killer, sheriff."

Parker placed his back Stetson back firmly on his head. "Maybe."

2

The bodies had all been naked. On their stomachs. Heads twisted around and facing backwards. Tongues extended with pentagrams cut into them. Exactly the same as what had happened in Diamondback. Only this had been in a Swiss forest at the foot of the Alps five years before. Gifts to Satan, his informant had told him.

A chateau was near the murder site. It was large and well-constructed, a place where the rich and powerful from Geneva and Bern liked to party. A man running his dog had seen flames and hooded figures and heard strange songs in a language he did not understand. There had never been a second opportunity for police to speak with the witness. The man and his dog had vanished and the chateau he lived in found neat and clean and empty.

Blackstone lay on his bed in the dark, praying, and thinking, and going over the day.

He hated to make it sound as if he were not a believer in supernatural evil. But it was one of the ways he distanced himself from Dirk Austen and his past as a hunter of sinister cabals rooted in the worship of the devil. Father Eric and Father Daniel, even the rabbi and the sheriff, had been disappointed with his response, their eyes had flickered in a certain way.

There is nothing I can do about it. That part of my life is over. What is happening in Diamondback is nothing more than a series of copycat killings. Someone, or a group of someones, has read a book about a Lucifer cult like Son of the Dawn. A neck is not so difficult to break using more than one pair of hands. Once that's done all those pairs of hands can work at turning the head around backwards.

"There has to be more than one murderer involved," murmured Blackstone.

The other question was why had they killed those particular men. Two drifters and a priest – the priest would be a far better sacrifice to Satan, so that was easy enough to understand. But had they got their hands on him because Father Henry had stumbled upon their secret society? Had his hunting trip been merely a guise to track the cult members to their ritual site? Or had it been they who followed Father Henry into the woods, looking for an opportunity to give his flesh and blood to the devil? And did they really believe in the Evil One or was it just a thrill, something they did high on crack or meth?

Blackstone recited The Lord's Prayer in English, Greek, Latin, and Aramaic and began to fall asleep.

Deliver us. Deliver us. Deliver us.

His cell phone burred. He had placed it on his bedside table next to his Greek New Testament. Its screen was lit up by the call.

"Hello?" he asked.

The cell phone clock said it was two in the morning.

"Pastor Jude?"

He recognized Sheriff Parker's voice. "Morning, sheriff. I hope you haven't called this early to tell me you have a new theory about the killings?"

The sheriff didn't laugh or apologize. "Meet me down at the morgue. Frank Lucas is dead."

Blackstone was at the morgue in ten minutes.

Father Eric was already there.

Rabbi Cohen arrived a few moments after Blackstone.

The sheriff and the coroner stood by the table where a body was draped in a sheet.

"Go ahead, Sam." The sheriff was pale. Even his dark green eyes looked pale to Blackstone. "Let's get it over with."

Sam drew back the sheet.

Frank Lucas was on his stomach. His head was wrenched around backwards. The tongue was pulled out past his chin and the pentagram had almost cut it in two. None of the blood from his tongue had been cleaned up. It covered the sides of his mouth and drenched the front of his chest.

"Who found him?" asked Cohen.

His black fedora was in one hand.

"The janitor at his church," replied Sheriff Parker. "Reverend Lucas was in front of the altar. The carpet is soaked in blood. I have a detective and two deputies there now."

"How long ago did this happen?"

"I would guess around midnight. Looks like Frank had been working late." Parker's face was rigid. "This will get out now. The janitor said he'd sit on the details but he's going to tell his wife. You can't keep something like that inside for long. It's too toxic. In forty-eighty hours the whole county will know. I've set up a press conference for tomorrow morning." Parker's hands turned to his fists as he gripped his Stetson. "There'll be the devil to pay."

The press conference was a zoo. News had traveled and affiliates of CNN and FOX and NBC were on hand along with journalists from as far away as Boise and Denver and Cheyenne. Sheriff Parker stood outside his brick office building flanked by four of his deputies and spoke about the murder of Frank Lucas. He called the other three deaths murders too. The manner in which each body had been mutilated linked them to the same killer. No, he would not be releasing any details about the mutilations. The FBI had sent agents in from satellite offices in Missoula and Bozeman. The case would be cracked, the murderer apprehended and brought to justice. Until then the citizens of Diamondback and the whole county needed to take extra precautions. If they had weapons permits they needed to go armed.

"His kids are only ten and eleven," Parker told Blackstone after the conference.

"I know that. I'm sorry."

"Do you think you and the others would come to his house with me? Talk to the boys and his wife and express your condolences? Pray with them?"

"I can't imagine Father Eric and Rabbi Cohen not joining us."

"I wish Father Daniel were here."

"He is," Blackstone said. "He drove in from Missoula. I just spoke with him."

"What about the Methodist minister? Brent Scott?"

"I'll give him a call."

Parker pulled a gold badge from his pocket. It was a star inside a circle. At the top rim of the circle the word CHAPLAIN was engraved. The bottom rim bore the words ANACONDA COUNTY SHERIFF'S OFFICE.

"I'd be obliged if you'd pin this to your jacket or shirt when you make official visits on my behalf," Parker said.

Blackstone took the badge. "I'd be happy to, sheriff."

"I have ones for the others too. It's an idea that came to me before the killings. Seems as if the Lord was getting me ready to deal with what was coming." Parker watched as Blackstone attached the badge to his denim jacket. "A badge suits you."

Blackstone did not reply.

There had been a partial boot print on the carpet by the body of Frank Lucas.

A trace amount of blood had formed its outline.

The FBI pointed out it was the same print that had been at the murder scene in the woods – a small notch on the tip of the toe proved that. Which meant the person wearing the boot had not just happened upon the victim in the forest and been too afraid to talk. Finding the print at the site of both crimes meant the person was either the killer or working with the killer.

"It doesn't add up," Parker complained. "We have a woman who can't be much more than five foot and one hundred and ten pounds tearing the heads off men a foot taller and twice as heavy. I don't care if she's the MMA female champion of the world, it doesn't figure."

"There could be three or four of them," Blackstone had suggested, presenting Parker with his theory. "That many could overpower anyone, break their neck, and twist their head around."

"Then where are their boot prints?" demanded Parker. "Why do we only see one kind of print at the last two crime scenes?"

"I don't know."

"One little woman doing all this. It makes no sense."

It didn't make sense to Blackstone either.

Not in terms of a straight up, five senses physical world.

Yet he found he was reluctant to cross the line and consider the other world. A world of spirits he knew intersected with the physical world all the time, an intersection that was sometimes subtle, but often as not spectacular with supernatural events, some that brought healing, and others that brought violence and death. Just because such a reality was no longer at the top of his "to do" list every morning, just because he was no longer ferreting out power cults 24/7, did not mean the dark forces those cults tapped into had gone anywhere. If the devil was real then the devil was still there and all his angels with him. And Blackstone knew the devil was real. In his life as Pastor Jude he might pass himself off as a man who only saw evil in the abstract, or as a dark aspect of the human soul, but that was a game to prevent people from knowing what he actually believed. In his real world, in his real mind, in real time, he knew evil had a face, a cunning, and a maliciousness that cut through human life like a black hell.

So Blackstone refocused.

In public, he continued to make it obvious that he loved God and loved people but did not believe a devil existed anymore than he believed the earth was flat.

In private, he acted the way he had acted for the past ten years of his life – he read the Bible in half a dozen different languages, prayed to God for guidance, watched for the telltale indications of supernatural occurrence, and left his mind open to what God might show him concerning the murders of Father Henry, Reverend John Lucas, and the two unknown men.

Let me see again, Father. Let me know again. Let me fight again. And in your power may I prevail over Satan and all the armies of the night.

A week after Blackstone had realigned his thinking and his vision, Reverend Brent Scott of the United Methodist Church was found dead at his desk in the church office. His head had been turned around until it faced backwards, his tongue was extended and a pentagram sliced into it, blood was on the desktop, his sermon notes, and the carpet under his feet.

There were no boot prints.

Blackstone fasted for five days, drinking only spring water. Nothing came to him, no words, no verses from Scripture, no visions. The Wednesday after Brent Scott's funeral he went to the gathering of ministers at the home of the Pentecostal pastor of Abundant Springs Church, Jack Slate. Everyone was on edge. They had each been approached by the FBI and the sheriff's deputies and warned about the pattern that appeared to be emerging – the killer was after men of the cloth. The murder of the unknown victims had either been for practice or to throw investigators off balance. Several pastors had carry permits and talked about the guns they now toted on a daily basis. A number of them had signed up for shooting classes at the indoor range. The fear made three or four feel the only way to deal with the threat was to shout their prayers as loudly as they could at the house meeting in order to show the devil they meant business. Others prayed quietly. Afterwards most of them lingered.

"How about your friends at the other ministerial?" Jack Slate asked Blackstone as they sat together in a corner of the living room. "How do they feel about all this?"

"They feel the same way the ministers here do."

"Not exactly the same," Slate corrected Blackstone.

"What do you mean?"

Slate glanced around the room. "Foursquare, Vineyard, Calvary Chapel, Baptist, Evangelical Free – these men believe there's a devil. Your friends don't."

"I wouldn't say that. Many of them just don't believe in ghosts and witches on broomsticks and demons lurking in closets. They don't want to see people use Satan as an excuse for the bad things they do or for all the wickedness in the world."

Slate nodded. "Sure, okay, we're accountable for our actions. But there is a tempter, there is a deceiver, there is a being that draws us into sin. Otherwise why would Jesus need to die on the Cross to save us? Couldn't we just save ourselves by our own efforts? But look at what we read in the Scriptures – *Be sober, be vigilant, because your adversary the devil, as a roaring lion, walketh about, seeking whom he may devour.* First Peter chapter five and verse eight. The Bible takes Satan seriously, Jude. The Bible treats him as if he's real, not a concept or a metaphor."

The Foursquare pastor, Wayne Gillespie, who was nursing a can of Coke nearby, turned to them. "But, to be honest, I can see where the pastors in the other ministerial are coming from, Jack. Some Christians wind up looking at the devil so much they can't see God anymore. There are demons of this and demons of that, spirits of Jezebel and spirits of witchcraft and spirits of rebellion. Pretty soon you're thinking more about what Satan is doing than what our Lord is doing."

"That's no reason to ignore the devil completely."

"Of course not. But what do you do with church members who think they're The Exorcist and go around casting demons out of half the people they meet and out of cars and fridges and stoves too? People make choices to do good or bad. Terrorists choose to use suicide bombers to blow up innocent people. Political leaders use torture and incarceration against anyone who tries to speak out against them. Serial killers like the one we're dealing with make up their minds that they're going to hurt and maim and destroy. You can't keep saying the devil made you do it.

Otherwise God could never judge you for the sins you committed. You wouldn't need Jesus to set you free of your past because you wouldn't be responsible for it. You're free of consequences if the devil put all the bad ideas in your head."

"Oh, he puts them there, Wayne," Slate argued. "But we act on them. That's why we have to answer to the Lord for what we do."

"All right. But I don't think he puts all of them there, hey, I don't believe he puts half of them there. I don't think the devil has anywhere near the power we give him credit for and I don't think he's doing anywhere near the damage in our churches or our cities that we keep saying he is. We do a lot of it on our own, Jack. It's human nature."

Slate laughed and clapped the Foursquare pastor on the back. "Human nature? You sound like one of the pastors at the other group. Maybe you ought to be showing up there instead."

Gillespie finished his Coke and shook the can to make sure it was empty. "Never been invited."

"You're welcome anytime, Wayne," Blackstone said. "First Wednesday of every month."

"Of course you'll have to put up with Jews and Buddhists and Catholics and what not." Slate's eyes on Blackstone were like snow and ice. "Not much chance to do Jesus praying there."

"You can do whatever praying you want," replied Blackstone. "No one is going to stop you from praying to Jesus."

"Or anyone else either – Buddha, Moses, the Pope."

"I've never heard anyone pray to Moses or the Pope or Buddha."

"Next you'll have Wicca in there and be holding a coven."

Blackstone shook his head. "No covens, Jack."

"Watch. You'll have female ministers before the end of the year. The Methodists will put one in to replace Brent Scott. God rest his soul."

"I don't care if they put in a woman minister, Jack. I just care that I'm free to speak and pray as I believe. And I am. That's no different than what we do here."

Color came into Jack Slate's face. "No different? Here we're all Christians. Here we all believe in the same God. You have no idea what the other ministers are praying to at your meeting."

"Those who believe in Christ will be praying to Christ. Their prayers will get through no matter what anyone else in the room is doing. What's wrong with that?"

"What's wrong with that is this is war. Holy war. Washington has turned against us. Our whole culture has turned against us. Satan and his demons are hammering at the gates. The Body of Christ is in retreat. We have to stop running, regroup, and fight back as one. As one, Jude. Not as a bunch of Catholics and Jews. As an army of believers in Jesus Christ our Lord. We don't have time for anything else."

"Well, Jack." Blackstone hesitated a moment. "It's amazing what God will do. Take a Jew and make him our Savior, for instance."

Slate ground the words out between his teeth – "Jude Blackstone . . . "

"I've been in worst case scenarios as a pastor where I counted on the Baptists and Pentecostals to say the right thing and they never said it, to do the right thing and they never did it, to walk in the footsteps of Christ and carry the Cross and they had absolutely no desire to do so. Then some Catholics came my way, and some Russian and Greek Orthodox, a few Episcopalians and United Methodists, and guess what? They followed the footsteps, they carried the Cross, they said and did the things God wanted said and done. You know what I learned from that? Our Lord works with people who have a willing heart not a denominational label. He doesn't care what's on your church sign. He looks into your soul and then he decides."

A smile came and went on Slate's mouth. "Nice speech. You're right about one thing. God knows the heart. He knows what people really believe. And that's how we're measured. That's how we're judged."

"All the same," Wayne Gillespie spoke up. "I'd like to sit in with you the next time the other ministerial meets, Jude."

"Love to have you."

Slate got to his feet. "You're wasting your time, Wayne. You won't see Jesus there. You won't see the devil you need to fight either."

"I don't want to see the devil." Gillespie stood up. He was a foot taller than Slate. "The way I hear it, he's vastly overrated."

3

Blackstone began to go out at nights and walk the streets.

He had no idea what the killer would look like, where an attack would be most likely to happen, or even if the attacker would be human.

If he spotted patrol cars, he slipped out of sight.

Or people. He did not want to frighten them.

For a week he went up and down empty streets, out of view of surveillance cameras, breath white in the cold, hood up, hands in the pockets of his North Face parka.

On the ninth night he stopped near a trash bin in an alley.

He had not heard anything with his ears.

But in his spirit there was a sound.

And a presence.

He turned and looked behind him.

A slender young girl in a white trench coat that was belted at the waist was standing one hundred feet away.

Her long brown hair was neatly combed and parted in the middle and her hands were in the pocket of her coat. She looked to Blackstone to be about sixteen. The girl's head was down but her eyes were on him. There was nothing unusual about the eyes. They were calm and brown like her hair.

In a moment she was gone.

Blackstone went to the spot where she had been standing.

Her boot prints were obvious in the light dusting of snow that had fallen at sunset.

The toe of one print had a notch.

She was not a ghost. She was not a spirit. Whatever she was she had human shape, and substance, and weight.

Two nights later she appeared behind him a second time.

He was on a path near the woods and hills.

There were no streetlamps.

He heard her sound in his spirit once again.

She had not needed light to be seen in the dark alley. And she did not need it here by the dark forest.

White trench coat. Hands in pockets. Hair parted neatly in the middle. Brown eyes fixed on his.

This time there was a message. It had no words but combined a sense of fragility with one of rage.

You are a prisoner, he said to her without opening his mouth. *It is not your anger. It is the anger of the one who has abducted you. I can help.*

She vanished.

Again the boot prints were there.

The next night she was far away and on top of a hill by a cluster of tall pine trees.

It was just like her previous appearances. She was obvious in her white trench coat in the winter blackness.

A plea came from her to him. Almost a whisper in his soul.

But the plea was devoured by a growl that was a tortured twisting of scarlet and black. It was a personal threat.

The next morning she was sitting on a chair by his bed watching him. White trench coat. Hands in pockets. Brown hair, brown eyes. In a moment she was gone.

When he arrived home that night she was at the kitchen table.

The plea was stronger. The growl louder and harsher with a snapping and biting.

Two nights later she appeared at his bedroom window.

Help me.

Kill me.

Then the face was no longer there.

A week afterwards he awoke to find her standing in the middle of the room staring at him. Skin, and trench coat, and snow boots were whiter than they had ever been. Her eyes seemed twice as large and they were also white.

I will take your head for the King of Hell. I will eat the heart out of your chest and spit your blood on the altar. All glory to Satan, all glory in the highest.

Her fingers touched his bare arm.

Even though both her hands were in her pockets.

Intense cold darted up his arm to his throat.

He began to choke and could not get a breath into his body.

I will take your head. I will take your head now. I will offer it up to the King of Hell.

Christ is my head, Blackstone fought back.

Your head is Satan's.

Christ is my head and I am his servant.

You are Satan's.

I am Christ's and I carry his Cross with him. His Cross. His Cross. His Cross.

The girl was no longer in the room.

Her fingers of winter were no longer on his arm.

His breath was no longer stopped in his throat.

Blackstone got up, put on his robe, knelt by his bed, and spent the rest of the night in prayer.

Towards dawn he laid his head on his folded arms and had a vision.

A tall dark man stood in front of him with his hands extended. In them he was holding flames that leaped and writhed. His face was both lit and shadowed by the fire.

"You cannot do this." The man laughed like glass shattering. "You followers of the broken god can never do these things. You do not have the power. I hold fire and I am not burned."

"You do not have the blood," Blackstone responded.

"Whatever blood we need we will pull from your wretched bodies."

"You do not have any blood. Angels do not bleed. Lucifer has no arteries or veins. He has no heart. But Christ has what you can never have, both heart and blood. The blood falls all over us and we are strong. It falls on your head and you die, you and the Already Dead One."

The fire went out in the man's hands.

Blackstone lifted his head from his folded arms.

Light rimmed the mountain peaks in his window with a brilliant silver.

"Where is she, Lord?" prayed Blackstone. "Show me."

He waited a moment and stood up.

Then did what he did every morning and evening.

Checked the small satellite phone hidden beneath a floorboard under a corner of the wall-to-wall carpet.

The phone the gray man in the white room had given him.

His touch made the phone glow and the screen brighten.

He spoke one word. "Preacher Man."

Colors swirled on the screen and patterns emerged. Then letters in Sanskrit. Blackstone thought in Sanskrit a moment and after that in English.

THANK GOD YOU ARE NOT NEEDED

He tucked the phone back into its hiding place and went to the bathroom for his shower.

Where is she, Lord? The Girl in White – where?

Two FBI agents from Bozeman came to his church office to question him an hour later.

When had Blackstone come to Anaconda County? Where had he been before that?

What did he think of Wicca? What did he think of devil worship? Was it real? Was it fake? Had he ever participated in a ritual?

How about his fellow clergymen? What did they believe about black magic? Did any of them think an actual devil existed? Or an actual hell? Did Blackstone?

How well did the ministers get along? Was there rivalry between the different churches and different denominations? Was everyone on speaking terms? Had he noticed any hatred between one pastor and another? Who was harboring grudges? What about death threats? Which men had uttered them even as a joke?

After five minutes Blackstone decided to distinguish between them by the names Bland and Blander.

"We understand there was a fight between Sheriff Parker and Reverend Lucas just before Lucas was killed." Agent Bland smiled at Blackstone. "Isn't that right?"

"No, that isn't right."

"Come on, pastor. Other witnesses say they quarreled and almost came to blows."

"I'm sorry; I don't remember it that way at all. Everyone was tense. We were in the morgue looking at the body of a friend whose head had almost been torn off. No one was feeling right. The sheriff and Lucas exchanged a few words; feathers got ruffled, but I never got a sense they were about to take it outside with fists swinging."

"Do you feel you need to protect Sheriff Parker?"

Blackstone felt heat come into his face. "I don't feel the need to protect anyone."

"Did you yourself have differences with Reverend Lucas? You know, divergent views on God and the Bible? Did those ever explode into arguments?"

Blackstone counted to ten and then spoke. "I have a meeting of clergy here once a month. Some are Catholic, some Orthodox, some Jewish. I've even invited the Buddhist and Bahai leaders. Precisely because I don't want us to fight one another – I want us to get to know each other and what each person believes. I don't want anyone hated or demonized for their faith."

"But it bothers you when other churches grow and yours doesn't." Agent Blander pitched in. "That must feel like a slap in the face. Make you angry at God. At the people who leave your church to go somewhere else. At the ministers who luck out with the bigger congregations. What an insult to you. I can't imagine what it would feel like to see Reverend Lucas' crowded parking lot and then glance out your window at the handful of pickups in yours."

Blackstone stared at them and suddenly burst out laughing.

Bland and Blander deliberately widened their eyes at him and made exaggerated faces of concern.

"Something funny about a serial killer, Pastor Blackstone?" Bland asked, also in an exaggerated way.

Blackstone knew it was time to bite his tongue but he could not stop himself. "You guys from Quantico really do live up to what all the other agencies say about you. Oh, don't act so surprised; I'm sure you know all those nasty words. Tell me, do you shoot all your rivals and bury the evidence? Have fights that end up with M4s slicing and dicing agents from the NSA and ATF? Hang guys from Homeland Security and the CIA from hydroelectric towers? Yes? No? Neither do clergy." Blackstone paused. "Or maybe you actually do kill all the field agents from those rival agencies."

The look on the faces of the FBI agents was no longer a mock one of exaggerated concern.

"What do you know about interagency rivalries, Pastor Blackstone?" asked Blander.

Blackstone leaned back in his chair. "I was a chaplain with the United States Navy for years. Didn't you Google that or check my file? I even ministered to the Navy Seals." He leaned forward across his desk, lowered his voice, and darkened his eyes. "Want me to bring them up to Montana to assist you with your investigation into the Clergy Wars?"

"We're not afraid of the Navy Seals." Agent Bland straightened his tie.

"I'm sure you aren't. I'm merely pointing out that just because different agencies have overlapping agendas it doesn't mean they kill one another because of it. Neither do clergy."

"We're all on the same side, Pastor Blackstone."

"Not today you're not."

The agents got to their feet at exactly the same moment.

"Thank you for your time, pastor." Agent Blander snapped his briefcase shut. "I'm sure we'll talk again."

Blackstone remained in his seat. "I'm sure we will."

"We'll show ourselves out."

"Please do."

Crystal poked her head in a few minutes later. "Make some new friends?"

"Apparently."

"Their faces didn't show much expression going into your office but they showed plenty coming out."

"I help people get in touch with their emotions. One of my gifts." Blackstone stretched. "Hold my calls, please. I need fifteen minutes of quiet prayer to clear my head and then I'm heading over to Big Sky Gym for a workout."

She smiled. "Body and soul."

"Body and soul."

Blackstone flipped through an English translation of the Bible, read a few of what he called his life verses that were marked in black pen, then settled back to let the words run through his mind and wait on impressions from God. Despite what he had read, and the direction in which he was inclined to take his thoughts, or what he was sure he needed to hear from God, a totally different phrase kept pushing in and dominating his meditations – *salvation is from the Jews.* As often as he thrust it aside it slipped right back into his headspace – *salvation is from the Jews.*

He knew where it came from. Jesus was talking to a woman in Samaria, a woman who had led something of a checkered life. They were sitting by a well, not just any well, an ancient well even in Jesus' day, dug by the patriarch Jacob. *You Samaritans don't know what you worship. But we Jews know what we worship because salvation is from the Jews.*

Blackstone swung around in his chair to gaze out the window at the mountains. They were white with fresh snow and small flakes were spiraling down out of the clouds to add more.

I have no idea what that has to do with everything that's going on here, Lord – salvation is from the Jews.

Finally he grabbed his gym bag and headed towards the church doors.

Crystal called after him. "Rabbi Cohen phoned."

Blackstone called back. "Did he say it was urgent?"

"He said he wasn't sure."

"I'll work out first."

The gym was half-empty. Blackstone waved to a few men and women but didn't engage in any conversation. He switched on his iPod, put in his ear buds, and began to bench press one hundred and ninety pounds, his warm up weight. A band that divided its time between Australia and Holland, The Sons of Korah, filled his head with their musical instruments, and their voices, and psalms from the Bible. He increased the weight, sweating and grunting and pushing with all his strength until, at three hundred and twenty-five pounds, he could only manage two presses before fighting the bar back into its cradle and collapsing. Even after listening to twenty minutes of the Sons of Korah the phrase from Jesus and Samaria continued to dominate his thoughts – *salvation is from the Jews.*

Blackstone tucked himself into a corner of the gym by the magazine rack and pulled out his cell phone. No one was within fifty feet. Super Max, one of the gargantuan local bodybuilders, was howling and roaring through his reps with three hundred pound dumbbells in each hand, so Blackstone was certain no one would be able to hear his phone conversation even if they were on top of him.

"Shalom, Rabbi John Cohen."

"John. It's Jude Blackstone."

"Ah. John."

"My secretary said you called."

"I did. But I don't know what to tell you."

"What do you mean?" asked Blackstone.

"I'm not your mystical rabbi," Cohen responded. "I don't spend hours crunching numbers looking for hidden meanings in their different combinations."

"You don't read the Zohar and you're not into Kabbalah."

"No, I'm not interested in any of that stuff. Excuse me, what is that ungodly screaming? Are you in a torture chamber?"

"That's Super Max. He's a Jay Culter and Arnold Schwarzenegger wanna be."

"You're at the gym?"

"Yes, hiding in a corner and letting Super Max drown out whatever we have to say to one another."

Blackstone could hear Cohen release a deep sigh.

"Listen," Cohen said, "I'll tell you what happened and you can make of it what you will. Have you ever heard of a golem?"

"Gollum? Like in Lord of the Rings?"

"No, not Gollum. Golem, G-O-L-E-M. It's a Jewish myth."

"Is it some kind of monster?"

"You tell me. There are dozens of different versions of the story. The one that's been haunting me for the past couple of days seems to be based on one from Prague in the sixteenth century. A rabbi creates a man out of clay, a huge man, and sets it loose to defend the Jews from pogroms, you know, anti-Semitic attacks."

"I know."

"His intentions are good but he loses control of the thing and it goes on a murderous rampage, killing friends of the Jews as well as their enemies."

"And you felt I needed to hear this?"

"It started with numbers swirling around in my head. Ones and nines and sixes and threes. I had a daydream about the numbers when I was reading the Tehillim, what you call the Psalms, and they formed themselves into a row, one-three-nine-one-six. So I tried to make sense of that in terms of what I was reading and came up with Psalm 139:16 which says that God *looked on my unformed body.*"

"So?"

"So," Cohen went on, "the phrase *my unformed body* is *galmi* in Hebrew, *my golem.*"

"Ah," Blackstone replied as Super Max shouted in triumph over a heavy weight he had lifted.

"And mixed up with all this is your face."

"My face? Are you suggesting that I'm a golem?"

"No, I think the idea is that we have a golem issue on our hands."

"The murders?"

"Yes, the murders."

"But why my face?"

"Well, you didn't have the Hebrew writing on your forehead that makes the golem come alive. So I believe we're being told Anaconda County has this golem thing going on and that you're supposed to deal with it."

"I'm supposed to deal with it? On my own?"

Blackstone could almost hear Cohen shrugging in his exaggerated way through the cell phone.

"Well," Cohen muttered, "I can't very well take this to the Sheriff's Office or the FBI, can I? *Excuse me, I have a lead on the serial killer, it's a person made of clay called a golem and it's responsible for all the broken necks and twisted heads in Anaconda County.*"

"But Father Henry and Reverend Lucas weren't anti-Semitic," protested Blackstone.

"Maybe it's not about anti-Semitism. Maybe it's about the golem fighting something else."

"By murdering innocent people?"

"I told you. In some versions of the legend the golem starts slaughtering all sorts of men and women. Or it could be that our golem story is about fighting Christians or the clergy. That would fit the murder pattern."

"If you're right and it kills you then we'll know it's not about battling Christians."

"Hey, good thinking. Are you asking me to walk around with a Star of David on my back to find out?"

"Of course you're clergy too; it could be after clergy, which would give it another reason to take your head off."

"Thank you."

"You're welcome."

Super Max screamed.

"You're not taking me seriously, are you?" complained the rabbi.

"As seriously as I can," Blackstone replied. "How seriously are you taking what you've told me? Have all these dreams and visions made you a convert to Jewish mysticism and the Kabbalah?"

"No."

"Me neither."

"But," added Cohen, "it was one of your own Christian poets who said, *God moves in a mysterious way his wonders to perform, he plants his footsteps in the sea and rides upon the storm. Blind unbelief is sure to err and scan his work in vain, God is his own interpreter and he will make it plain.* I affirm these words. I affirm the entire hymn."

"So you really think there's a golem running around and God wants us to deal with it?" demanded Blackstone.

47

"God wants *you* to deal with it. Look, I don't get it, Jude, I don't get it at all. But if I have any sort of meaningful relationship with the God of Abraham, Isaac, and Jacob, then I believe he put all these numbers and images in my head and that they are pointing to the horror we're dealing with in Diamondback. And that he's also telling me you have some sort of unique professional background or lifetime of experience that equips you to deal with it. Remember the old MASH show on TV? *That is all.*"

"Bless you, rabbi, you've made my day."

"Bless you in return, my son, it's off my shoulders and onto yours."

"God may ask you to lend me a hand."

"I already have."

"Is that what you call it, rabbi? Dumping all this weird on me?"

"I can't listen to the shrieks of agony from your gym anymore. See you at the ministerial."

Cohen ended the call.

"Sure," Blackstone said into his silent phone. "*Salvation is from the Jews.*"

No matter how much he prayed and asked for insight or for dreams and visions, no matter how many hours he pored over the Scriptures or Googled the golem legend, Blackstone did not come to any earthshattering understanding of what Rabbi Cohen had told him in terms of the killings they were dealing with. While he wrestled the matter through, each day that went by he expected to hear about another murder or that the FBI had started to arrest various clergymen, but there were no more murders and no arrests. The Girl in White did not appear to him on the winter streets he walked at night anymore. And at the ministerial at Blue Sky Baptist Church in March there was a marked easing of the tension and fear that had been gripping them since the killing of Pastor John Lucas.

"Thanks for inviting me," Wayne Gillespie told Blackstone after the half hour of prayer. "I find myself as free to express what I believe in with this group as I do at the meetings at Jack Slate's house. With the added benefit that I don't have to put up with the ghost hunters attitude that's so prevalent."

Blackstone handed him a cup of coffee and a donut. "But you believe in demons?"

"Sure I do. But Jack and some of the others have them coming down the chimney."

"Have you ever done any deliverance ministry, Wayne?"

"No, it's never landed in my lap, thank goodness. I know it goes on but some of the guys on TV I've seen do it make me sick; there's so much hype. The devil's out there; evil's out there, but the less said about it the better. If I did have to do some exorcism stuff I'd do it on the quiet. It wouldn't be like some halftime show at the Super Bowl."

Blackstone took a drink of his coffee. "Good."

"You're not a big believer in the devil anyways, are you?"

"Not much."

"But you'll head back to the ministerial at Jack's place next week, won't you?"

"I will."

Gillespie finished off his donut and wiped his hands with a paper napkin. "Well, if he asks, you can tell him I won't be back."

A week later Jack Slate did ask and Blackstone told him what Gillespie had asked him to say.

"Won't be back?" Slate's face was pinched with anger. "Why? He didn't like the coffee?"

"I think it had more to do with what he considered an overemphasis on the work of the devil."

"Overemphasis? Is that how you see it?"

"I'm just telling you where Wayne is coming from."

It looked to Blackstone as if Slate was going to spit. "So he hangs out with unbelievers at your church meeting but he won't sit and pray with solid Christians under my roof? Is that it, Jude?"

"He said he felt free to pray to Christ at the Blue Sky ministerial."

"Oh, he did, did he? So what about you? Why are you still coming here?"

"I feel free to pray in both places."

"As I recall you don't think much of the devil either."

"Am I supposed to think a lot of him?"

"You're supposed to believe in him and his wicked ways."

"I believe a lot of evil is done in his name, is that good enough?" Blackstone noticed a tall man he had never seen before sitting and talking with a number of the pastors. "Who's the suit?"

Slate, anger still cutting across his face, glanced back over his shoulder. "Oh, that's Frank Markham. He's minister from Helena. Non-denominational church. He came down to minister to our congregation while we're going through this crisis."

"Is he staying with you?"

"For now. We have plenty of room. Mary's been with the Lord three years and my two boys are living in Denver."

"What about Sandy?"

"She's homeschooling. Her decision. One year left. Her cousin Alicia is staying with us from Seattle. They're doing all the course work together. Makes this big old house less lonely."

"Glad to hear it."

"Well." Slate turned away. "Frank is going to share before we pray and eat. I should ask him to get started."

"I'll just use the washroom. I'll be right back."

"There's one downstairs and to the right if this one's busy."

Two of the pastors were already lined up and waiting for the one on the main floor so Blackstone headed down the carpeted staircase. It was also in use. He sighed and sat down on a nearby couch and picked up a copy of TIME. The wait wasn't long. He'd barely read an article on the war in Syria when the door opened and a teenage girl came out.

"Hey," she said but didn't smile.

"Hey," Blackstone replied.

Their eyes met.

She didn't move and neither did Blackstone.

It was the Girl in White.

Only her hair was dark red.

And she wore jeans and a hoodie instead of a trench coat.

But her eyes were still brown.

And she still wore her hair parted in the middle.

"I'm Alicia," she said. "Did we meet already?"

"I don't think so," Blackstone replied. "I'm Pastor Jude from the Baptist church."

"Oh, maybe my uncle's mentioned you."

"Maybe. How's the homeschooling going?"

"It's awesome. Sandy and I are acing everything."

"That's great. Have you been here since the school year started?"

"Yeah, I showed up in September. My home's in Seattle." She smiled. "Well, I'd better get back to work. Nice meeting you."

"See you," replied Blackstone.

Alicia opened a door and he heard another girl ask, "Who were you talking to?"

"One of your dad's pastor friends."

Alicia shut the door behind her.

Back upstairs the pastor from Helena talked about the devil and how he often came as an angel of light, but only part of Blackstone's mind was with him, a very small part. The larger part was racing with thoughts and prayers and trying to make the connection between the redheaded Alicia and the brown-haired girl in the white trench coat who appeared to him on the dark streets of Diamondback. No solution presented itself. He did not pray out loud when the time came. Nor did he stay long to eat lunch with the other ministers. He shook a few hands, introduced himself to the visiting pastor Frank Markham, and headed back to his church office. Crystal met him in the hallway. Her eyes were flat and her face colorless.

"What is it?" asked Blackstone. "What's wrong?"

"Weren't you at the meeting at the Pentecostal minister's house?"

"I'm just getting back from it now."

"And they didn't tell any of you anything?'

"Tell us what?"

"The Sheriff's Office called ten minutes ago. The Foursquare pastor's body was discovered this morning in a trash bin downtown. The same thing all over again – broken neck, twisted head, cut up tongue." Crystal looked like she was going to faint. "When will it end, Pastor Jude? What's going to happen to us? Why is this killer stalking Anaconda County?"

His mind suddenly numb and empty, Blackstone hugged her. "It's going to be all right. This won't go on forever. God is bigger than this killer. He's going to get us out of this."

She pulled back and stared into his face, dark circles under her eyes. "How, pastor? How?"

A hard-edged wind was coming down from the mountains the day they put Wayne Gillespie in the ground.

There was a crowd at the cemetery, including the mayor and councilors, the Lieutenant Governor of Montana, FBI field agents, Sheriff Parker and his deputies, and hundreds of members of churches and other faith communities including Buddhist and Bahai. Blackstone stood with Crystal and her husband and other members of his congregation at Blue Sky Baptist. Pastor Gillespie's closest friend, Brett Sanders of the

Vineyard Fellowship, took the service in the Big Country Hall and at the graveside.

"I am the Resurrection and the Life," Brett said, standing tall in his Marlboro Man shearling jacket in the icy wind. "Those are the words Jesus used at Lazarus' grave. And they are just as appropriate here. Wayne Gillespie is alive in Christ. His body has returned to the earth out of which it was formed, but his soul is free with the Lord of heaven and earth. Evil may hurt the body. It can't hurt the spirit of a man who has given his heart to Jesus. Pastor Wayne is safe and secure. His murderer is not. Nor is the devil that propels that murderer to do his wicked deeds. Both will answer to God for what they have done. There will be a day of reckoning. Oh, yes, there will be a final judgment for the evildoer and his false god. And that moment is not far off. Our city and our county must hold together and believe that. Our city and our county must put their trust in the power of the Father, Son, and Holy Spirit. If we do that together, and persist in our faith in God, this reign of terror will come to an end."

Sanders went on to praise Gillespie for his ministry to the Foursquare church and the community. Blackstone looked over the faces in the crowd. He recognized most of them. Jack Slate's friend, the non-denominational minister from Helena, stood head and shoulders over the people around him. Next to him was Jack and next to Jack was his daughter Sandy who Blackstone had only met two or three times. And right beside Sandy was the Girl in White except she was dressed in a black Patagonia fleece with white detail, not a trench coat. But the detail matched her white snow boots that were the same ones Blackstone had seen her, or some sort of unholy version of her, wearing whenever she appeared to him on the streets or in his house. Her face was stony and her eyes fixed on Sanders. She never looked at Blackstone.

People were leaving, cars were starting, Blackstone held back before approaching Gillespie's widow and children and offering his condolences. After he had spoken with them, he took up three handfuls of frozen earth and snow and dropped them on the casket that had already been lowered into the ground. Under his breath he spoke a brief prayer in Latin.

Deus, et ulcisar.

God will avenge.

"What's that about?" It was Rabbi Cohen. "Three handfuls. Some sort of Trinity thing?"

"Yeah, some sort of Trinity thing."

Cohen put up the collar of his long black coat. His black fedora was firmly on his head. "Death is always hard but winter makes it worse."

"Some people tell me they find blue sky and sunny weather that much crueler when they've lost a loved one. As if death were mocking them."

"I can understand that."

"John, come over this way with me, will you?"

"Why? What's up?"

"I want to be sure you can say we both saw the same thing. If there's anything to see, that is."

"What are you talking about?"

Cohen followed Blackstone to the edge of the trampled snow that surrounded Wayne Gillespie's grave. Blackstone had his head bent and was looking closely at the ground.

"What are you expecting to find?" asked Cohen.

"A boot print."

"In this mess? The snow is all churned up."

"It seemed to me they were standing on the very edge of the crowd of mourners. She might have been right on fresh snow the whole time."

"Who's she?"

"The golem."

"What?"

Blackstone went to one knee. "Look at that. They were right about here and even with all the prints a bunch stand out. She must have walked away through the clean snow when she left."

Cohen leaned over. "What am I looking at?"

"The small boot prints. Do you see the notch in the toe?"

"If I try hard. Yes, I can see it."

"That same boot print was found at two of the murder scenes."

"Three, Pastor Jude."

Blackstone looked up quickly and saw Sheriff Parker. "Where did you come from?"

Parker went to one knee beside Blackstone. "I was curious and followed you. Had no idea what you were up to, but I had a hunch it might have something to do with the case. Not sure why I thought that." He examined the boot prints. "They were in the alley by the trash bin. Where we found Wayne Gillespie's body. Two sets of them." Parker looked around the cemetery. "Everyone's gone but the backhoe operator. He'll start filling in the grave shortly." His eyes came back to rest on Blackstone. "So are you going to tell me who was standing here?"

"Jack Slate and his daughter Sandy and two house guests – a visiting pastor named Frank Markham and Sandy's cousin Alicia."

"How old is this Alicia?"

"I'd say about seventeen."

"Okay. And who do you think was wearing the boots – Sandy or Alicia? Or was another teenage girl standing nearby?"

"It's Alicia."

"How can you be sure, pastor?"

"It's Alicia."

Parker got to his feet. "I guess I'll go have a talk with the family. You two like to tag along?"

"Right now?" asked Rabbi Cohen.

"No time like the present." Parker paused a moment as the backhoe roared to life. "Do either of you happen to have your chaplain badges in your pocket?"

"I have mine," replied Cohen.

Blackstone stood up. "Never leave home without it." He opened his hand to show the badge.

"Well, pin them on. Perhaps it'll help." Parker took off his black Stetson and ran a hand over the stubble on his scalp. "Better pray before we go there too. Something tells me we'll need all the help we can get. I don't expect it to go well."

The backhoe rumbled towards the grave and scooped up a bucketful of dirt. There was a loud thundering as the earth tumbled into the grave and struck the casket. Blackstone let the other two go ahead of him after a quick prayer together. He spent several minutes watching the machine operator work quickly to cover Wayne Gillespie's body.

4

Parker had been right. The word prescient also came to Jude Blackstone's mind.

The interview at the Slate home did not go well.

Pastor Jack Slate was not happy to see Blackstone or a Jewish rabbi when he opened the door. He was even less happy when Sheriff Parker asked to see Slate's daughter Sandy and her cousin Alicia. The visiting pastor, Frank Markham, joined the group in the living room and was soon responding to the sheriff's queries as if he were a member of the family.

"Pardon me," Markham interjected at one point, "but I get the impression you think this family, and these girls in particular, are somehow involved in the murders that have been plaguing Diamondback for the past few months."

"Just asking questions, sir," responded Sheriff Parker.

"It's preposterous," Slate growled. "This is a Christian home and Sandy and Alicia are young Christian women. How on earth could you think they knew anything about the murders or the murderers?"

"Any help or insight they or you could provide would be greatly appreciated."

The girls stared at the sheriff with blank expressions on their faces.

"I don't know anything about the killings," said Sandy.

"Sorry." Alicia now had purple streaks in her red hair. "Neither do I."

"Can you tell me where you both were on the night Pastor Gillespie was killed?" asked Parker.

"What?" exploded Slate.

Markham shook his head. "I see where this is headed. Do you really think two teenage girls could twist a man's head off?"

"I want to know if they were out walking and saw anything," responded Parker.

"They weren't out walking and they didn't see anything!" Slate almost shouted.

"I'd prefer to hear them say that themselves, Pastor Slate."

Markham shook his head a second time. "If I were you I'd call my lawyer, Jack."

"I was thinking the very same thing!" snapped Slate.

"There's no need to bring in lawyers," Parker protested, "I'm only looking for information."

Blackstone got up. "Excuse me a moment, I'll just the use the washroom."

He went down the stairs, into the washroom, flushed the toilet, and ran the tap water. After that he opened the door to the girls' room. It was messy, clothes were everywhere, Justin Bieber posters covered the walls, laptops were on both beds. He looked in the closets. The first one was jammed with hoodies and tee shirts and jeans and leather boots. The second had coats and dresses. One coat was in a blue plastic dry cleaning bag. Blackstone lifted up the bottom of the bag. The bag covered a white trench coat. To the side he noticed a pair of white winter boots resting on a rubber mat.

"I think you missed the door to the washroom."

Blackstone turned to face Frank Markham. "Seems that way."

"What are you looking for?"

"Just curious."

"Curious about a clothes closet? You don't act much like a pastor."

"I could say the same thing about you."

Markham smiled. "Let's cut the crap. Who are you with?"

"The Baptist church."

"On the surface maybe. But I smell Dies Irae. If I pinned you down and ripped the clothes off your back would I find a tattoo of the tetragrammaton?"

"Why stop with my clothes? Why not tear off my head?"

"We tried. We'll try again."

"You won't win, Markham. Or whatever your name is."

"Of course we'll win, Blackstone. Or whatever your name is."

"The goat's head and pentagram behind your left ear is pretty obvious, don't you think?"

"Only to someone who's looking for it. It's pretty small."

"But speaks volumes."

Markham had a Glock pistol in his fist in an instant. But his speed was matched by Blackstone who was suddenly pointing a Heckler and Koch semi-automatic at Markham's head.

"I could shoot you now and be within my rights," said Markham.

"Me, I'd just claim self-defense."

"Who would the court believe?"

"They wouldn't believe you. You'd be dead."

"Maybe not."

"Hey, you're already dead, Markham. There are some verses about the followers of Satan in the Book of Revelation. You come to a nasty end."

Markham curled his lip. "Propaganda. The war's far from over."

"The Cross. With broken arms. Suspended upside down."

"Because your crucified god is a powerless fool."

"If he's so powerless why do you put the ring around the broken Cross?"

"You know why we use the rings."

"To keep power inside the circle. To keep it from getting out and harming anyone you don't want harmed. Especially the ones who are summoning up the demons and casting the spells."

"That's right."

"If Christ is powerless why encircle his Cross? Or is there something you're still afraid of, Markham?"

"Blackstone!" It was Parker calling down the staircase. "You taking a shower? Time to go!"

Blackstone kept his gun on Markham. "Be right up!"

His eyes and Markham's eyes remained locked.

Blackstone lowered his pistol to his side but did not holster it.

"Be seeing you around," Blackstone said as he walked up the stairs.

"Sooner than you think," Markham promised, his Glock still on Blackstone.

Parker saw Blackstone slip his gun into a holster concealed under the waistband of his jeans. "What was going on down there, pastor?"

"I'll explain outside."

"I sure hope you have a permit for that thing."

"I do. Signed by you when I first arrived here in 2012."

"What is it? Looked Heckler and Koch, HK."

"Yes, sir. HK USP 45."

Jack Slate was standing by the open door. "You're not welcome here from now on, Jude. Not you or Sheriff Parker or the Jew."

"I'm sorry to hear that, Jack," replied Blackstone. "The rabbi and I were only trying to help with the investigation. You do want the murderer caught, don't you?"

"Not at the expense of accusing two innocent girls I don't."

Rabbi Cohen was leaning against his car, his breath white in the cold March air. "I guess there are no Jack Slate meetings in store for this clergyman."

Sheriff Parker had his hands on his hips. "Blackstone here was pulling a High Noon downstairs. With a German made 45 pistol."

Cohen snapped up straight and looked at Blackstone. "What?"

"He drew first," said Blackstone.

"Who?" demanded Parker.

"Markham."

"The pastor from Helena pulled on you?"

"He's no pastor. He's a devil worshipper. Belongs to a cult group called Dark Angel."

"Markham told you that?"

Blackstone touched his ear. "There's a tattoo back here."

"You were going to shoot him based on a tattoo?"

Blackstone held up his hands. "Trust me. He's part of a big, bad cult. They have cells in every nation you can think of. I doubt he's in Anaconda County to help us lick our wounds."

"What are you saying?" Parker tugged his Stetson down more firmly on his head. "You think he's the murderer?"

"I believe he's involved in the killings, yes."

"And Jack Slater?"

"I'm not sure. He may not know anything about Markham's secret life. But I found the boots in a closet the girls share."

"Were they the ones?"

"Markham showed up before I could look."

Parker puffed out his cheeks and exhaled a mouthful of air. "I need to get a warrant."

"To search this house?"

"What else? If we find the boots the girls will have to stop playing innocent."

"Markham's onto us. He saw me going through the closet. The boots will be gone." Blackstone blew on his hands. "We need to be at Abundant Springs Pentecostal Church tonight. It's just a hunch."

"What's going to happen at the church?"

"A ritual. Markham will believe he has more power there."

Parker frowned. "Why would a person you say is a Satanist believe he has more power in a church?"

"He's going to desecrate it. The same way they desecrate the Roman Catholic Mass with a Back Mass."

"I thought you didn't believe in that stuff," Rabbi Cohen said.

"I don't. They do. That's why I think Markham will go to the church. He's pretty certain you'll return here with a warrant to search the premises. So he'll be at Abundant Springs instead."

"Why not just stay here at the house and hide the things he doesn't want us to find?" asked Cohen.

"Because he wants to enact a ritual. And he wants more power to do it. A desecrated church provides that. He said he'd tried to kill me once. Now he's going to try again."

Parker stared at him. "He tried to kill you once? Were you attacked?"

"Psychologically. Spiritually. Never physically."

"That's the point," said Cohen. "I thought Satanists were mostly about self-empowerment and worship of the ego, worship of the self. A lot of them don't even believe in an actual devil, do they?"

"That's one movement," replied Blackstone. "But the killer in Diamondback isn't that kind of Satanist."

"No, I suppose not."

"I'd like to have you there, John."

"Where? At the Pentecostal church? I don't believe in black magic any more than you do."

"All the better. Markham can't frighten you."

"His gun might frighten me."

"I'll have guns there." Parker looked past Cohen and Blackstone at a mountain peak emerging from a cloud. "But I hope you know what you're talking about, Blackstone. The whole thing sounds nuts."

"What about the murders, sheriff? What do you think of those?"

Parker grunted. "What time are we meeting at the church?"

"The witching hour. Three in the morning."

"Three! Why is that the witching hour?"

"It's when evil ridicules the Holy Trinity, the Christian teaching of Father, Son, and Holy Spirit. It's also the opposite of three in the afternoon which is when Christ died on the Cross."

"Whoa." Rabbi Cohen opened the door to his car. "Time for this Jewish boy to head home. But I'll be at the church. It sounds like I'll be impervious to almost everything that happens there."

"That's what I'm counting on," replied Blackstone.

Parker and Blackstone watched the rabbi drive away.

"How weird is it going to be, pastor?" asked Parker. "On a scale of one to ten."

"Pretty weird, sheriff. For you it will be off the scale."

"Well, then, I'm going to bring in a lot of heat. I hope you're right about this."

Blackstone opened the door to his Jeep Rubicon. "It's just a hunch."

There would be an attack on Blackstone well before three in the morning.

He knew how Dark Angel worked.

He prayed and read Scriptures in Greek and Hebrew and Latin and prepared.

Then he settled himself in a straight back wooden chair he'd picked up at an antique dealer and waited.

When the roaring and snarling began it was distant and sounded like two dogs fighting.

It grew louder and came closer.

Cold swept Blackstone's body and it was accompanied by an overpowering desire to let go and fall asleep.

The roaring and snarling became so loud it threatened to enter him and obliterate all his thoughts and beliefs.

He began speaking the name Jesus in Latin, Greek, and Hebrew, the same names nailed to the top of the Cross on which Jesus died.

Despite the roaring, and the cold, and the longing for sleep, he continued to repeat the names.

Suddenly there was a burst of music. It flowed through Blackstone's head. Rich and melodic, it sounded like a hymn, but he could not recall which one.

The roar ended immediately.

Blackstone's eyes had closed during the attack. He opened them.

"Thank you, my God," he whispered.

He recited the 101 Vow out loud, one of the oaths of the Dies Irae. It was Psalm 101 and ended with the words, *Morning after morning, I shall reduce all the wicked to silence, ridding the Lord's city of all evildoers.*

After that he put on a CD of hymns in Latin. The tunes and words were a thousand years old. Monks and nuns were singing them while he prayed and meditated.

An hour later he pulled up behind the sheriff's patrol car. It was parked a block away from Abundant Springs Church.

"You ready, pastor?" asked Parker.

"I am. Is it just you and two deputies?"

Parker nodded. "Carson and Selleck are all we need."

"Where's the rabbi?" asked Blackstone.

"No idea." Parker checked his watch. "We'd better get in there if you want our arrival to coincide with that witching hour of yours."

"Not my witching hour. Let me pray a moment, sheriff."

Parker removed his Stetson. So did his deputies.

Blackstone blessed them. After that they walked towards the church.

The front doors were open.

The hallway was dark except for the red glow of an EXIT sign.

Blackstone could smell candle wax and smoke and incense.

"We should check the sanctuary," he whispered to Parker. "Something's going on here."

"Go ahead," said Parker in a low voice. His pistol was in his hand.

Blackstone swung open the heavy wooden doors.

Black candles were burning in a circle around a black pentagram that had been chalked on the carpet. The chairs that normally filled the space were stacked to either side. In the center of the pentagram Alicia stood facing Blackstone in her white trench coat and boots. Her hair was red with the purple streaks and parted in the middle. But her eyes were gone. There were no pupils, just flames.

Help me.

Kill me.

I will tear the head off your neck and eat the heart out of your chest.

Blackstone whispered, "Jesus is greater than all the darkness that has consumed you. He will set you free."

"That will do, Blackstone." Markham walked out of the shadows dressed in his suit. "No cries to your god for her liberation, please."

"What's going to stop me?"

"A bullet to the brain." Markham smiled. "He carries an HK, sheriff."

Parker pressed the barrel of his pistol into the back of Blackstone's skull. "I know. Drop it on the carpet, pastor."

Blackstone slowly unholstered his pistol and bent to place it on the floor.

"Did I tell you to do that?" snarled Parker.

"I may need it again, sheriff. I can't let anything get broken by a fall."

"You won't need it again."

Jack Slate stood up from a chair in the far corner of the sanctuary. "We can't seem to kill you by means of our devil girl. A bullet will have to suffice. But a bullet is good and right. Anaconda County will wake up to find the killer was caught by the sheriff and shot resisting arrest."

"What did you do to Alicia?" asked Blackstone.

"There is a spirit in her. You would call it malevolent. We consider it benevolent." Slate's face suddenly twisted in a burst of rage. "It did not have to go this way. Alicia came to me with a troubled soul. She was tormented by a rogue demon. I needed help to cast the demon out. That was when I realized how few of my fellow clergyman believed in the devil and in his fallen angels. I complained about this lack of faith on one of my chat groups online. That was when I met Reverend Markham. Or rather Bishop Markham of the Order of Lucifer Dark Angel."

"Let me guess," responded Blackstone. "He suggested you teach the clergy a lesson and use Alicia as a vessel of retribution. It would be a win-win for both of you – you would see faithless ministers of the gospel punished and teach the others a lesson about the truthfulness of Scripture. Markham would have sacrifices for Satan, wonderful ones, Christian clergy. He could also see if the spirit in Alicia could be harnessed in such a way as to become a hit man for the devil. It seems to have turned out well for you both."

"You think too much." Markham was standing directly in front of Blackstone. "I suppose I shouldn't expect any less from a member of Dies Irae. Shoot him and let's be done with this piece of Christian trash."

"A bullet in the back won't look good," argued Parker.

"Turn him around then."

Once Parker put his hand on him, Blackstone caught it, bent it back, broke it, took the sheriff's Glock, and put three shots into Markham's head, certain he was wearing body armor under his suit.

"Strike, Destroyer, Strike!" yelled Slate.

Alicia gave a shriek and sprang from the pentagram.

She landed in front of Blackstone in a crouch, her young face rippling with dark lines and snarls, the flame in her eyes a vivid crimson. She reached her hands towards him, once, twice, but was repelled each time. With a howl of rage that made the windows in the sanctuary shake, she pounced on Sheriff Parker who was standing right behind Blackstone and cradling his broken hand. He screamed as she seized his head in her hands and jerked it viciously to the left. Everyone heard the snap. Shouting words in Latin that Blackstone could not make out, Alicia yanked Parker's head around in a complete circle. Then she paused to spit in his eyes and give it a final twist so that his head faced backwards. Letting him collapse to the floor, she bent over him, turned him on his stomach, pried open his mouth, extracted his tongue, and using a knife from the pocket of her trench coat, cut a pentagram into it.

"No, no, no!" cried Slate. "Destroyer, obey me! Stop!"

Alicia got up and slapped Slate so hard across the face that he staggered and fell.

"Why should I obey you, Christian?" demanded Alicia in a rough and dark voice. "I am of hell. Your god is not master there."

She sprang on Slate and dug her fingers into the sides of his head.

"Suppose now that it is you who die, that it is you who are the sacrifice?" She laughed. "You will not go to the heaven you love, not after all the evil you have done. I will dispatch you to my Master in hell. Oh, it has been a very good season of blood here in Montana."

The deputies looked from Blackstone to Alicia, their guns out.

"Did you think you could control this force at will once you unleashed it?" demanded Blackstone.

"Markham promised us," Selleck said.

"Markham was of his father the devil. And the devil is a liar."

"No, no, a lesson," sobbed Slate as Alicia's finger grip began to draw blood. "It was only meant to teach the ministers and all the churches a lesson. A lesson that would bring them closer to God. Then the demon would leave Alicia and us. That was what we all agreed upon."

"You cut a deal with the devil!" snapped Blackstone. "And now you have the devil to pay!"

"Blast her head off!" shouted Carson to Selleck. "The deal's over! Blow her away! We'll call up another demon!"

"FBI! Lower your weapons!"

Men in helmets and tactical gear began running into the sanctuary with M4 carbines ready to fire. Selleck and Carson spun around. Selleck dropped his pistol right away but Carson took aim and let off several rounds. Shots were returned and Carson was hurled against the wall and a stack of chairs. Blackstone tackled Alicia but her strength was enormous and he could not pin her. She punched him twice in the face, drew blood, shrieked and clamped his head between her hands like a vise.

"Third time's the charm," she rasped and tightened her grip.

Her crimson eyes flared.

Blackstone stared directly into them. "I order you in the name of Jesus Christ – crucified, dead, buried, and risen again – to come out of her."

Alicia hesitated.

"Do it!" shouted Blackstone. "Now!"

"Ahhhhhhhhhhhhh!" Alicia flew backwards and began to convulse. Then she lay as still as stone.

"Was she hit?"

Blackstone recognized Agent Bland of the FBI even with his helmet and goggles on.

"No," Blackstone replied. "She had a seizure. Get your Tac Med to look at her."

Bland spoke into a microphone attached to the uniform on his chest. "Medic. Up front." Bland looked at Blackstone. "You okay?"

"I'm good."

"Can you tell me what the heck is going on here?"

"Ritual abuse. Black magic. Harnessing evil spirits to commit murders. Devil worship. The usual FBI case load." Blackstone made a jerking motion with his head. "Better cuff Pastor Slate. He was behind this. Deputy Selleck too. No point in shackling Markham."

Bland glanced around him. "Who shot Markham?"

"I did."

"You like head shots or something?"

"I was afraid he had body armor on."

"Are you undercover, Blackstone? Because you smell like undercover to me."

Blackstone paused a moment. "Dies Irae. But I'd rather you didn't make that public knowledge."

"Dies Irae? You're kidding me. That's like saying Wil Smith and Tommy Lee Jones are going to walk through the door with a little red light and tell us they're from Division Six."

"I'd show you my badge but it's in my other pair of pants."

"I hear they're pretty cool."

"They're black and gold and glow in the dark."

"This sounds like so much crap, Blackstone. Let's see the tattoo. You do have the tattoo, right?"

Blackstone lifted his right hand from his prone position on the carpet. Keeping his fingers together he only separated the little finger from the ring finger. Bland crouched and took a good look. On the inside of the ring finger, small but perfectly and precisely formed, he saw:

יהוה

"No way." Bland grinned. "That's the tetragrammaton?"

"It is."

"And it's God's holy name? Like, his personal name?"

"Right."

"How do you pronounce it?"

"There are a lot of corruptions. The correct form is to say Yahweh."

"I have to tell the guys about this. There really is a Dies Irae. There really is a secret agency called Day of Wrath."

"Open your mouth and you'll violate the Espionage Act and a whole lot of other Federal statutes that can land you in prison or maybe on a table with a needle in your arm."

"Oooo. Touchy."

"Complain to the Pope. And the President. I can give you a list of the others, but I doubt you'll have much luck with them either."

Blander had shown up and was cuffing Jack Slate.

"I demand to see my lawyer," cried Slate. "I'm within my rights to ask for him."

"Shut up," said Blander. "You witch doctor."

"I'm a minister of the gospel."

"You're an apostate. Isn't that the word, Reverend Blackstone?"

"That's the word."

Blackstone caught Deputy Selleck's eye as the FBI led him away. "Why?"

Selleck shrugged. "There was money in it. And power."

"And murder. And the devil."

"You were supposed to be the last death. You and the rabbi. The devil would have his due, Slate the lesson he wanted to teach the other ministers, Parker and Carson and me our sack of gold. Then Markham and the devil girl were supposed to leave and everything return to normal."

"Once you let the devil in nothing returns to normal, deputy."

"I never believed in Satan and all the demon nonsense Markham and Slate did."

"Do you believe in him now?"

Rabbi Cohen, Father Eric, and Father Daniel walked up as Blackstone climbed to his feet.

"Are you hurt?" asked Cohen.

"A few scratches. Glad you three got my message. I'm even more glad you were able to twist the arms of the FBI."

"It wasn't so hard," replied Father Daniel. "They had their suspicions about the Sheriff's Office already."

"What tipped you off, Jude?" asked Cohen.

"When I mentioned the tattoo of Dark Angel. Parker started playing with his Stetson. Which made me take a closer look at his left ear, the location where they always mark their own. I have to say I was surprised. I didn't think he'd cross the line."

"There are all kinds of reasons people cross the line," said Father Eric. "Jack Slate doesn't look too repentant about his crossover."

"I would say he gave up his soul a long time ago. Now he doesn't even notice what he's done." Father Daniel watched them drag Slate from the sanctuary, still arguing and protesting. "But he wasn't the only one harboring secrets. I thought you didn't believe in the devil, Jude Blackstone."

"I said that just to cover up another life."

"What other life?"

"I was a vampire hunter."

"A vampire hunter?" Cohen smiled. "You mean like Buffy?"

"More like a combination of Blade and Van Helsing. I wanted to leave all that in the past."

"And then this happened in Anaconda County," said Father Daniel.

"Yes. This happened."

"What about the girl?" asked Father Eric. "And what about Jack's daughter?"

"They'll need prayer. They'll need counseling. A good amount of that counseling needs to be grounded in the love of God. I was hoping some of you would get involved."

"Who decides?" asked Eric.

"I have no idea. Child Protective Services?"

"Won't the girl that did the killing go to trial?"

Blackstone nodded. "I expect she will."

"What about the demon?" asked Cohen. "I saw you cast it out. What happens to the demon?"

"It finds another home." Blackstone's face was dark. "It finds another vessel to live in."

EPILOGUE

"I remember things."

"What things?"

Alicia shrugged. "Seeing you on the street. Seeing you in your house."

Blackstone nodded. "Do you remember what happened the night at the church?"

"A little. I know I was hurting people."

"In time, by the grace of God, most of those memories will heal."

"Even in prison?"

"Even in prison. But I don't believe you'll be there long even if you are convicted. And there's the very real possibility you won't be found guilty of murder. Not if the jury believes that your father and Frank Markham were controlling you."

"No one will believe the devil was running my life. It will be just like *Emily Rose.*"

"You never know." Blackstone squeezed her hand. "I'll always be praying for you. If they want me to testify, I'll testify. If you're in prison, I will visit you as often as I can. And I know some great prison chaplains. You'll never be alone."

"Pastor." It was Agent Bland standing by the doorway of the coffee shop. "It's time."

"All right."

He stood up just as Alicia did. Her hair was blond and curly and not parted in the middle. They hugged.

"Christ bless you," said Blackstone.

"You too." She held a ceramic coffee cup in her hand. "Do you think I can take this with me? Like a memento or something?"

"Go ahead. I'll cover it."

He walked her to the door.

"Thanks for the extra time, J. Edgar." He smiled at Bland.

"No problem, Reverend."

They shook hands.

"If you're ever by the Missoula office, drop in," Bland told him. "Just don't bring any of the weird stuff with you."

"I won't. I hear Missoula has plenty of weird stuff as it is. Especially among the Feds."

Bland led Alicia to a dark blue Ford Galaxy. Blander was at the wheel. He gave Blackstone a thumbs up.

Blackstone went back inside, paid for the ceramic coffee cup, lingered a bit and finished his own coffee and soup, left, got into his Rubicon, and drove to his house. Four packages were on the doorstep. One was a brass menorah from Rabbi Cohen, another a carved wooden crucifix from Farther Eric, the third a painted icon of Jesus with brooding eyes from Father Daniel. The last package he opened was from Crystal and it was a freshly baked apple pie. He hung the crucifix and icon on the wall and placed the menorah in an alcove in the brick wall by the fireplace. The pie he put in the oven. After it was warmed up, he cut himself a generous slice, dropped a scoop of vanilla ice cream beside it, turned on the gas fireplace, and sat with plate and fork in an armchair, eating the pie, and watching orange and yellow flames race back and forth.

I shall sing of loyalty and justice as I raise a psalm
*   to you, Lord.*
I shall lead a wise and blameless life.
When will you come to me?
My conduct among my household will be blameless.
I shall not set before my eyes any shameful thing.
I hate apostasy and will have none of it.
I shall banish all crooked thoughts and will have no
*   dealings with evil.*
I shall silence those who whisper slanders.
I cannot endure the proud and the arrogant.
I shall choose for my companions the faithful in the
*   land.*
My servants will be those whose lives are blameless.
No treacherous person will live in my household.
No liar will establish himself in my presence.
Morning after morning I shall reduce all the wicked
*   to silence*
Ridding the Lord's city of all evildoers.

Blackstone went to his bedroom, peeled back a corner of the carpet, lifted a floorboard, and pulled out the small satellite phone the gray man in the white room had given him.

"Preacher Man," he said into the phone.

After a moment the screen lit up and letters in the Hebrew alphabet emerged and arranged themselves. Blackstone read the message and returned the phone to its hiding place. He stretched out on his bed, thinking he would get up in a minute and change out of his clothes. In an instant he fell asleep while the March sky darkened outside his window.

THANK GOD YOU ARE NOT NEEDED

www.ingramcontent.com/pod-product-compliance
Lightning Source LLC
Chambersburg PA
CBHW051926220626
47052CB00003B/601